NAILS

★ ★ ★ ★

A Boy at Bunker Hill and Valley Forge

★ ★ ★ ★

by Richard M. Bowen

with illustrations by Nathan Goldstein

PROLOGUE

Nails of Bunker Hill, whose real name was Paul Lewis, was taken off a captured ship by a pirate and given the nickname "Nails" because of the way the small boy had fought when captured. He was rescued by some seamen who had stopped for supplies at the Island of Tocca in the Caribbean, and smuggled aboard their ship. Brought back to Boston, he was left to shift for himself.

Nails was taken in and befriended by a gunsmith named Mr. Baldwin, who was a militia leader. At the battle of Bunker Hill, Nails saved Mr. Baldwin's life and was wounded himself while bringing ammunition to the defenders. A British officer who met Nails on the hill called him a hero of the battle, and later on in a London newspaper, while writing his memories of the battle, he mentioned a boy, "Nails of Bunker Hill." This article helped Nails locate his real parents.

PART ONE: BUNKER HILL

Chapter One

AFTER a long voyage, the crew of the Brig *Havens-pride* was very happy to get ashore at the small island of Tocca in the Caribbean Sea to take on fresh supplies for the last leg of the journey home to Boston. It had not been the most happy voyage, and a state of war had existed most of the trip between the ship's first mate, Isaac Simms, and Captain Greenledge, with the crew taking sides almost to the point of mutiny.

Mate Simms went ashore with part of the crew to purchase fresh vegetables and supplies and to load barrels of water. But after months of salt on their lips, they stopped at the local inn called "The Leg in Irons" for some ale and rum.

The Island of Tocca had long been a pirate island, but in past years the island had had a steady stream of legitimate trade ships and men of war seeking out the pirates, so the pirates had wisely moved to more secluded islands for their own protection. A few remained, calling themselves retired pirates, who said they had given up their careers of violence. They made their living by selling fake maps to buried treasure and slitting an occasional throat over a shilling or two.

"The Leg in Irons" was a hangout for these retired pirates.

At the inn Mate Simms, standing at the bar with his men, announced that he would buy the first drinks, and as time went past many more were consumed. Simms and his men were laughing and singing, but through the merriment he noticed a young boy going back and forth to a table, carrying drinks. He had a collar around his neck with a chain attached, and if the drinks were not brought back fast enough, the man at the table would pull the chain almost to the point of snapping the boy's neck. It was the cruelest thing that Simms and his men had ever seen, but everyone else in the inn seemed to ignore it.

"Innkeeper," said Simms, "who is that man and who is the boy?"

"Blade Griggs," answered the innkeeper. "He is a former pirate and the boy is his bought-and-paid-for slave. Griggs is a dangerous man and has killed at least four men that I know of who were trying to free the boy. Because of that and because there is no law on the Island, nobody else has tried to free the boy, even though we all think that he is being cruelly treated."

"Well, warships stop here — why don't you tell them about Griggs and they will free the boy?"

The innkeeper said, "Everytime the ships come here he takes the boy and hides in a cave."

"Well," said Simms, "in good conscience I could not leave here and see the boy remain in the hands of that villain."

Turning to his men he said, "Perkins, I want you to go back to the ship and bring back my sword. While we wait I will try to figure some way to get the boy away from Griggs without one of us getting killed."

Simms noted that Griggs was sitting with his back to the wall, the table in front of him, and that he had a sword and a pair of pistols on the table.

"In that position he could kill two men before we even reached the table," Simms said. "I think our best plan of attack is to start a fight among ourselves in front of his table to distract him. Cox, you will get knocked down in front of his table. Then I want you to crawl up against the table and throw it back against him. Then we will all jump him at once."

Cox asked, "Shouldn't we wait until Perkins gets back with your sword?"

Simms answered, "No, I don't think I'll need it with this plan." Then he said to his men, "Mind you, be careful of the boy. If Griggs decides to pull hard on the chain, it will break his neck."

The fight soon started as planned, and Cox was knocked to the floor. Griggs viewed the fight with great pleasure. This was something he liked and he relaxed. At that moment Cox pushed the table over and down on him. But Griggs, giant of a man that he was, just pushed the table back on Cox, trapping him under it. Griggs' pistols however, were knocked on the floor and away from him. At this point the boy slipped away from Griggs. Griggs, enraged, pulled out his sword and headed for the rest of the crew, who stood paralyzed with fear, realizing that their plan to trap this man behind the table had failed.

Suddenly Perkins rushed into the Inn and handed Simms his sword.

Griggs snarled, "I'll cut you into little pieces," and headed right for Simms. Simms quickly picked up a stool and warded off Griggs' first thrust, which cut halfway through the stool. This caught Griggs' sword just long enough for Simms to thrust his own sword forward and kill Griggs. A loud cheer rang out from the Inn. It was like David killing Goliath all over again. Simms was the hero of the day.

Simms looked for the boy and found him huddled in the corner behind some barrels.

"Boy," he called, "Don't be afraid. Come out here."

The ragged little form stepped out from behind the barrels.

"Come here, son, and let me take off the collar and chain. What's your name?" asked Simms.

"I don't know, sir," answered the boy. "I was very young when he took me and I can't remember my real name. Griggs called me Nails. He gave me that name because I fought so hard, biting and scratching him when he took me off a ship that was captured by pirates. Everyone on the ship was either killed or walked the plank. Griggs was the pirate ship's First Mate and they let him keep me as part of his share of the loot. He had a monkey as a mascot, but he threw him overboard because he could not keep two pets. He said he was sorry he ever did it because I was worth less than the monkey. The monkey could at least swing by its tail."

Simms asked Nails if there was anything by which he could be identified.

"The only thing left is in Griggs' pocket. It is a chain with a medal on it that he took from around my neck."

Simms walked over to Griggs' motionless body and reached into his pocket. He pulled out a fine silver chain with a medal on it. He examined it carefully and, turning it over, found the initials P.L. on the back.

Simms placed the chain around Nails' neck, saying, "If you ever find out who you are, it will be this chain and medal that will identify you."

Chapter Two

"WELL," Simms said to his men, "we've got a problem greater than saving Nails."

"What's that?" asked Perkins.

We have to get him aboard the ship without Captain Greenledge finding out."

"Why don't we put him in one of our water barrels, nail it up, and take him aboard that way?" suggested Cox.

"Good idea," said Simms. "Let's get to it."

Captain Greenledge stood by the rail watching Simms and his men approach the ship in the longboat, loaded with barrels and supplies to the point of sinking.

"Simms," said Captain Greenledge strenly, "what took you so long? Spent most of your time in an Inn, did you? Get those supplies on board. I want to sail with the next tide," and with that the Captain left the rail for his cabin.

"Well, that's a break," said Simms. "No one will be watching while we load."

Nails was bumped around quite a bit in the barrel, but the thought of being saved eased the pain. Finally everything was stored safely in the hold, including Nails. It was a great relief to him when Simms pulled off the end of the barrel. The sudden surge of air, even though it was stuffy, felt good.

Simms said, "Now listen carefully, boy. We have weeks of sailing ahead of us before we reach Boston. We will bring you food, water and a blanket. You will have to stay in this hold, hidden behind these barrels. We will have a signal whistle. If you hear someone coming who doesn't whitsle, climb right into this barrel and stay there until you are sure he is gone. I'll put a piece of rope in the barrel top so you can pull it back down when you get inside, and I'll drill a peep hole so you'll be able to see out of it. Nails, your safety on this ship depends on your following my instructions. Is that clear?" asked Simms with a stern tone to his voice.

"That's very clear," answered Nails, "and I will try to be as careful as I can. Thank you very much, sir."

The first week was very uncomfortable for Nails. He became seasick and could not eat for the first few days. Simms worried about his young charge and on occasion took Nails on deck in the middle of the night when Cox was standing the watch. The seasickness passed and Nails began to get his sea legs.

The hold was not as stuffy and hot as it had been in the tropics, for the ship was sailing north and the cool breezes were something new for Nails, who had spent so many years on Tocca. Nails' shivers brought to him something he had longed for while he was a prisoner of the pirate. Simms gave him his old mate's coat, which hung like a nightgown on him, but was his proudest possession.

One night Nails awoke because of a great lurching and crashing around him. The ship was heaving and shaking violently with water pouring down ladders and hatches. The barrels in the hold had broken loose and were being tossed in every direction. Nails leaped to the nearest ladder to get out of the way of the moving cargo. He hung onto the ladder for dear life, cargo crashing around his feet. After what seemed like hours, his arms were so tired that he thought he could not hold on any longer.

Suddenly the hatch opened above him. It was Simms.

"Good boy," he said, "hang on. The Captain asked me to check this hold. It has been my first chance to get off the deck since this Northeaster hit us. I'll get a length of rope and tie you to the ladder. This is going to be a rough one to ride out."

Simms tied Nails securely to the ladder. Nails thought to himself how lucky he was to have such a friend as Simms. He could not have hung on to the ladder a moment longer and surely would have been crushed in the hold.

Gradually the storm subsided and everything grew quiet, but Simms did not come. Finally the hatch opened. It was Cox. He untied the ropes around Nails and Nails dropped to the hold and crawled over to his corner, which was littered with broken cargo.

Cox followed and said, "I have bad news for you, Nails. We have lost a friend. Simms was washed overboard during the storm while trying to clear some rigging on the deck."

Nails started to cry.

"Now, son," said Cox, "Simms was a good sailor and he died like one. I know he would not want you to cry over him. I'm First Mate now, and I'll take care of you the best I can. We'll have to find you a spot back farther in the hold. The men that I bring down here to clean up will be ones who know you are here."

Nails, who for the first time in his life had felt happy and secure, even though a stowaway, felt helpless and alone. The loss of Simms to him was like the loss of a father.

In a few weeks the battered ship reached Boston.

Cox came down into the hold and said, "Well, Nails, we're home. I don't know what I can do with you. I'm a sailor. I go ashore, get drunk, and then sign on another ship. The best I can do for you is this."

He handed Nails some coins.

"Here's some money. I owed it to Simms. I know he would have wanted you to have it. The cook has given me some food for you."

He handed it to Nails who wrapped it up in a piece of cloth.

"The Captain's gone ashore so I'll get you off the ship now," said Cox.

The sunlight almost blinded Nails after the darkness of the hold. The air was cold, the coldest he had ever felt. Even Simms' warm coat didn't seem to keep the cold out.

There were ships, people, carts, and horses everywhere. Nails stared at civilization with great surprise.

Cox walked about two blocks away from the waterfront with Nails and stopped outside a sailor's tavern.

He said to Nails, "You are on your own, Nails. There are lots of good people here in Boston. You have food

and a little money. Someone will help you when it's gone."

Cox turned abruptly and went into the tavern.

Chapter Three

NAILS felt alone and sad at losing another friend, but the excitement of being in Boston and seeing so many new things helped him forget his loneliness. Buildings and shops, the hustle and bustle of the streets, all left Nails' neck sore from trying to take in all the sights at once.

For hours Nails wandered down streets and up alleys until he found that it was getting dark and he was hungry. Nails saw a very comfortable looking barn. The door was not locked so he went in. It was dark inside. He was startled by a noise, but it was only two horses in their stalls.

He saw a ladder leading to a hayloft above and thought it would be safe and warm in the hay, so he climbed the ladder and made himself comfortable. He unfolded his sack and ate the stale ship's food which Cox had given him. After eating, he looked around and found an old horse blanket, covered himself with it and was soon fast asleep.

He was suddenly awakened by loud noises and shouting. He looked down from the hayloft and saw one man on a horse trying to ride out of the barn and another man hanging on to his leg trying to pull him off.

The second man was shouting, "Stop thief! Get off my horse!"

In the excitement and darkness, the only light being the moonlight shining through the open barn door, Nails fell out of the loft and landed in a pile of soft hay inside a stall. This startled the man who was trying to stop the thief, and the thief, tumbling off the horse, ran as fast as he could out the barn door.

The man, thinking that Nails was the thief's accomplice and was trying to steal his other horse, rushed into the stall and grabbed Nails. Nails did not know why this man was attacking him, so he fought like the name he had been given by the pirate. Finally Nails was subdued.

"Why," said the man, getting a good look at him, "you're just a boy. I thought you were a bobcat. Why were you trying to steal my horses and who was your accomplice?"

"I don't know who that man was," said Nails, "and I was not trying to steal your horses. I only came in here to get out of the cold to sleep."

"I don't believe you," said the man.

"It's true!" said Nails.

The man said, "My name is Mr. Baldwin. Come into my house so that I can see what you look like in the light and listen to your story. Mind you, boy, don't you try to get away," and with a firm hand on Nails' shoulder, Mr. Baldwin escorted him into the house.

It was a warm and comfortable place, thought Nails, as Mr. Baldwin ushered him in front of the fireplace and told him to sit down on a bench. He offered Nails some tea. Nails accepted and the warmth of it made him feel better.

"Now, boy, let's hear your story, and it had better be the truth."

Nails talked for hours, telling Mr. Baldwin about the pirates and Simms, and showed him the silver chain and medal.

Mr. Baldwin said, "Boy, this is the strangest story I have ever heard, but I believe you. You have had a terrible time. I don't know what I can do with you, but I hate to think of turning you over to the authorities. They would put you in an orphanage and you don't deserve that after all that you have been through.

"I live here alone. My wife and my only son, who was about your age, died of the fever a few years ago. I am a gunsmith — some say the best, although I know that hasn't been true since my family was taken.

"I'll tell you what, boy. I'll let you stay and live with me on a trial basis. You can help around the house and you can work with me in my shop as my apprentice."

"I would like that," said Nails without any hesitation.

"Remember," said Mr. Baldwin, "this is a trial. If you don't behave or aren't willing to do your share, out you will go."

Nails said, "I'll try my very best."

Chapter Four

AS TIME passed, living and working with Mr. Baldwin gave Nails a happiness and sense of security that he had never felt in his life. Each day was a new experience. Mr. Baldwin's great patience and kindness made things very easy for Nails. He even took one hour off in the middle of the day to give Nails reading, writing, and arithmetic lessons, with time in the evening for more.

Nails learned to ride on Mr. Baldwin's horses, and had the use of Jeff, a black horse with a white face, which Mr. Baldwin's son used to ride. He had bought it for a birthday present the year the boy died and, because his son had loved the horse so much, he just couldn't bear to part with it.

Mr. Baldwin had been in deep mourning over the death of his family, but now, with Nails living and working with him, he noticeably began to be his old self. The company of Nails was doing as much for him as it was for Nails.

One of the things Nails liked best was to ride with Mr. Baldwin to hunt game into the countryside. Mr. Baldwin was an excellent rider and a crack shot. Of all the new things that Nails was learning, riding and shooting were his favorites.

In this year of 1775 there were great stirrings in the Colonies, and Boston was a center of opposition to the taxes and injustices of the English king who ruled the Colonies from thousands of miles away. Mr. Baldwin was a great supporter of the cause of liberty and independence, and on many nights he had meetings at his house. He and his friends discussed and debated ways of obtaining independence from the Crown — even to the point of arming themselves and driving the British out of Boston.

In the sixth month of Nails' stay with Mr. Baldwin, a sense of excitement gripped Boston. The day was April 19, 1775. The British had marched to Lexington and Concord looking for arms and supplies and rebel leaders. On the Lexington green a small group of farmers, warned by the ride of Paul Revere and William Dawes, had stood their ground and been fired on. Eight Colonists were killed and ten were wounded.

As the British continued their march to Concord and back to Cambridge, farmers all over the area rose to arms and fired from behind trees, walls, and windows. By the time the British reached the safety of Cambridge they had lost 247 killed and wounded, and compared to 88 American casualties. These figures were quite a shock to the British, who had at that time about the finest troops in the world. They knew that these farmers with long rifles, shooting with deadly accuracy from behind barriers into their rigid military formation, were something new to be reckoned with.

The excitement of this clash brought into the open all

the hostility between the Colonists and the Crown. Mr.
Baldwin's house was the center of more and more activity. Meetings were held almost every night. Militia groups
were being formed all over Boston, and Mr. Baldwin,
who had had some military experience in the French and
Indian War, was one of the militia leaders.

Great amounts of powder and shot were being stored
in Mr. Baldwin's cellar, and on certain days he and his
company would meet outside Boston to drill and shoot at
targets. Nails would go along, driving a wagon with
water and food, and acting as the company cook. On certain days he would act as a runner, like Paul Revere before him, going to all the houses, alerting the militia company to form. These days were very exciting for Nails.
He was very proud of the duties given to him. He felt
he was a part of this great cause for which so many good
men like Mr. Baldwin were ready to lay down their lives.

There were many drills, but in mid-June, 1775, the
British, under General Gage, wanted to strengthen their
fortifications around Boston. Nails' ride on this day was
not a practice drill. The company, along with many
others, were to march and fortify Bunker Hill and resist
any attempt of the British to take it. After he had alerted
all the militia, Nails returned to Mr. Baldwin's house
where he was told to drive a wagon load of shot and
powder that would be needed in defense of the hill. Nails
worked along with the company, fortifying the hill and
making many trips with the wagon to bring up supplies
and water.

When the British troops started to embark from their

ship and the ship's guns started to bombard Bunker Hill, Mr. Baldwin told Nails to go back down and stay far enough away to make sure he would be safe should the hill be overrun by the British. Nails tried to talk Mr. Baldwin into letting him stay. Mr. Baldwin was firm, so Nails left and watched from a distance.

As the great assault started he could see the waves of redcoats climbing the hill with murderous fire tearing into their ranks. It was a slaughter. Twice the British assaulted the hill and were driven back in disorder. By this time small groups of wounded militia were staggering down from the hill.

One of the men fell and Nails helped him up. He had a terrible gash in the side of his head and he was weak from loss of blood.

Nails asked him, "How is the battle going?" and to Nails' surprise the man answered, "Badly! We are almost out of powder and shot. I don't know how we can stop another assault."

Nails was shocked. He had thought the battle was going well for the militia. Then he remembered that in the wagon Mr. Baldwin had some horns of powder and shot which were kept under the seat for hunting — three bags of shot and five horns of powder. Nails thought that this ammunition would be needed.

Taking the powder horns and the heavy bags of shot, he put them around his shoulders and he started off at a fast pace up the hill. When he reached the top he was shocked at the number of dead and wounded

lying everywhere. He had never seen anything so terrible in his life and he felt frightened.

He searched among the thinned ranks for Mr. Baldwin and his company. Shots were whistling, men were dropping here and there. Suddenly Niles felt a sharp pain in his leg. When blood trickled down it he realized he had been hit. It did not hurt badly — the leg was just a little numb — and he could walk on it although it pained him.

At last he found Mr. Baldwin, who was not happy to see him, but was glad to get the powder and shot. "Nails," he cried, "you get down the hill as fast as you can!" He also looked at Nails' leg and said, "You're a lucky boy. It isn't serious."

Just then the third assault started and shot filled the air. Most of the militia were out of powder. Mr. Baldwin pointed to a mound of sand and logs and said to Nails, "Get over there and stay behind it! Keep down as low as you can. It is safer there than going down the hill with all this shot in the air."

The British assault reached the top of the hill. The militia fought with fists and rifle butts, for their ammunition supply was gone. From his hiding place Nails watched the battle. He saw Mr. Baldwin fall. He immediately got up and ran over to Mr. Baldwin, who was badly wounded.

"Nails," he said, "hide and save yourself!"

"I can't leave you," said Nails.

By this time most of the militia had retreated and the British were all over the hill. A big burly soldier approached and was going to bayonet Mr. Baldwin. Nails picked up a discarded British rifle and drove the bayonet on it deep into the back of the soldier's leg. The soldier fell forward with the rifle dangling from his leg. Then, enraged, he pulled it out and lunged at Nails with the same bayonet-tipped rifle, dripping with his own blood.

Just then a heavy red-coated arm came down on the rifle, knocking it aside. It was a British officer.

"Sergeant," he said, "it's bad enough that we are fighting farmers without trying to kill a boy."

"But sir, he bayoneted me."

Nails said, "I was only trying to stop him from killing Mr. Baldwin."

"You're a good soldier, boy," said the officer to Nails. "What is your name?"

"It's Nails, sir."

"Is that your real name?" asked the officer.

"Sir, I am an orphan. I don't know my real name."

As the officer left he said, "You're a hero, Nails of Bunker Hill."

People began to swarm all over the battlefield, picking up the dead and wounded. They helped Nails to load Mr. Baldwin into the wagon along with other wounded. He drove them to the barn on a doctor's property where they were treating the many wounded. People from all over were bringing in bedding and bandages and helping.

Mr. Baldwin was gently taken off the wagon and brought into the barn. It was dark and Nails was tired. He found some feed and fed the horses and then soon fell asleep in the back of the wagon. He was awakened by one of the women who were helping the doctor.

"Are you the boy that brought in Mr. Baldwin?"

"Yes, I am," answered Nails.

"The doctor says you can take him home. He said he will be all right and that he will mend better in his own bed. Why, boy," said the woman, "what's the matter with your leg? Did you cut yourself?"

"I was shot on the hill yesterday."

"You were in the battle?" she asked.

"Yes, ma'am," answered Nails.

"You poor child, get down off there and come in to see the doctor."

The doctor cleaned and bandaged Nails' leg.

"It isn't serious, boy," the doctor said, "but if it were not properly taken care of, it could have become infected."

Nails and Mr. Baldwin were taken home and put to bed, and some of the neighbors came in to take care of them both.

Chapter Five

NAILS was up and around the next day, but Mr. Baldwin's wounds would keep him in bed for many weeks. One of the people that came in to help them was Mrs. Woods, a widow. She said she would stay on as a temporary housekeeper until Mr. Baldwin was better.

Mrs. Woods was a good cook and just as good a housekeeper, and the house began to shine. Each meal was something to look forward to. In the evening Mrs. Woods would play the piano and sing. She had a wonderful voice and sang regularly in the church choir. Her singing in the evening, after a delicious meal, was as much a dessert to Mr. Baldwin and Nails as the apple pie they had just eaten.

One morning there was a knock at the door and Nails answered. The man standing there asked him, "Are you the Nails that was at the battle of Bunker Hill?"

Nails, surprised, replied, "Yes, I am."

The man said, "I am Mr. Fowler, and I own a newspaper. I want to show you something."

He took a newspaper clipping out of an envelope. He said that it was from a London newspaper which had been sent to him by a relative. The story was written by an English officer who had been at Bunker Hill and it told about the battle.

Mr. Fowler read the story to Nails. In it the officer mentioned meeting a boy named Nails who was wounded and who had heroically saved the life of a fallen man. When he had finished reading he said to Nails, "You are a very well-known boy in London. I would like to write a story about you for my newspaper so that the people around Boston and the Colonies will know about you."

Nails said, "I will have to talk to Mr. Baldwin and get his permission first."

Mr. Baldwin heartily agreed and they all sat down that evening while Nails told his whole story from his first recollections of living with the pirate. Mr. Fowler said that it would make a fine story and would appear as the feature article in his next week's paper.

The interview by Mr. Fowler and the coming story in the newspaper made Nails feel very excited. Knowing this, Mr. Fowler sent the first copy off the press to Nails. Nails asked Mrs. Woods to read the paper out loud to him and Mr. Baldwin. Nails was not, as yet, a good enough reader to understand all the words.

Because of the article many people started coming by to see Nails and he was constantly being pointed out on the street. But one person reading the article in Boston dropped the paper after reading it and said, "I don't believe it, but it's true." The man, Colonel Lewis of General Washington's Army, which had been newly formed in Cambridge, said to himself, "This Nails is my son. He

is the right age, and the description of the medal with his initials on it proves it."

For years the Colonel and his wife had thought their son had died at the hands of pirates. He wanted to go right away to see Nails, who, after all these years, was only a few miles away. But he thought of the pain that his wife back in Philadelphia had suffered at the loss of their only boy, and knew that the reunion should be made together. With General Washington's permission, he rode day and night to Philadelphia. He returned to Boston with his wife by carriage, a servant doing the driving so that the Colonel could get some rest.

Nails was in the barn catching up on some neglected chores when Mrs. Woods, in a loud voice, called, "Nails, come into the house right away." Nails, thinking that Mr. Baldwin had fallen out of bed or something worse, ran to the house where he was confronted by an officer and a lady, both of whom were crying.

Mrs. Woods, who was also crying, said, "Nails — I mean Paul — these people are your mother and father."

Nails could not believe it. He was hugged and kissed and hugged some more. When the excitement quieted down they all sat down to supper and Colonel Lewis related the story of how they had bought a plantation in the Indies and could not take Paul with them because he had come down with a fever just before the planned departure and was too weak to travel. His aunt had agreed to bring him by ship later on when he was stronger.

"We found out that the ship had been sunk by pirates. One man had escaped by playing dead when the pirates were on the ship and when it went down he clung to some wreckage. He said that no one else had survived. We were heartbroken at the loss of our son, so we sold the plantation and moved to Philadelphia."

Nails was very happy and excited at finding his real parents, but was sad at the thought of leaving his friend Mr. Baldwin alone and going to Philadelphia.

Mr. Baldwin, sensing something wrong with Nails, said, "I have an announcement to make. Mrs. Woods and I are going to be married."

A broad smile broke over Nails' face and he ran over and kissed Mrs. Woods, who hugged him. The announcement stopped Nails' fears about Mr. Baldwin being left alone, and made him feel better.

Colonel Lewis, knowing the great affection that Nails must have for Mr. Baldwin, said, "Paul, you can visit with Mr. Baldwin any time you want. You will not lose your good friend, just because you are going to Philadelphia."

"Yes," Mr. Baldwin replied, "I will be your uncle from Boston."

The next morning, with sad farewells but a happy heart, Nails started on his journey home.

PART TWO: VALLEY FORGE

Chapter One

I
T WAS a long and dusty journey back to Philadelphia, but Nails enjoyed every mile of the trip. Sitting
between his parents made him feel as comfortable as if
he were on a thousand pillows.

Arriving in Philadelphia, Nails said, "Why, it's as big
and as beautiful as Boston. I can hardly wait to see our
house."

"I hope it will please you," said Mrs. Lewis.

"Well, we're home," bellowed Henry the coachman.
Nails looked with wonder at the splendid big brick house
before him. It had a high fence around it and spacious
lawns.

"How do you like it, Paul?" asked Colonel Lewis.

"I think it is beautiful," said Nails, quickly hopping out
of the carriage, almost knocking over Henry who was
trying to help Mrs. Lewis out. Nails kept repeating,
"This is the most beautiful house I have ever seen."

Colonel Lewis said, "You haven't even seen the inside
yet."

A man opened the front door and said, "Welcome
home, Master Paul."

"Thank you," said Nails, who was very impressed by
his white-toothed smile and handsome red uniform.

"I am John, the butler," said the man, taking a bag out of Nails' hand.

Colonel Lewis said in a joking manner, "Paul, John is the boss around here, next to your mother. You ought to see him chase the neighborhood children out of the side yard with a broom when they start climbing our apple trees."

John laughed and said "Don't let your father talk you into thinking I am a villain. I only chase them as a last resort if I think they are going to ruin the trees." Nails laughed.

Inside the house was a broad white spiral staircase leading to the upstairs. "Come, Paul," said his mother and father, "we will show you to your room."

"I am anxious to see it," said Nails.

Mrs. Lewis went ahead and opened the door and led Nails into the room. Nails just stared at the wide canopied bed, the carpeted floor, lamps, paintings on the wall, and a huge fireplace. He thought to himself how different all this was from the way he had lived with the pirate.

"What do you think of it, Paul?" asked Colonel Lewis.

Nails was speechless. Tears filled his eyes as he answered "Fine." He walked over to his mother and father, who were standing together, and hugged both of them at the same time.

Colonel Lewis pulled out his handkerchief and wiped a tear away, and then said, "Well, family, I am hungry. How about you?"

"I am starved," said Nails.

"Agnes, the cook, told me she had our supper ready

when we got home and it must be on the table now. Yes, I can hear her ringing the supper bell."

The meal was delicious and soon after eating, the family, exhausted by their long trip, went to bed.

A few days later Colonel Lewis said, "Paul, you have had little formal education. Your mother and I have enrolled you in Mr. Black's boys' school. Things will be hard for you there at first because you have years of education to catch up with. I have talked to Mr. Black and explained your situation to him. He said that you can go to regular classes with the other boys, but you will have to be tutored here at home in the evening by his assistant, Mr. Willis. It will be hard for you, Paul, but I know you can do it."

"I'll try my best, Father," said Nails.

The next morning he went off to school, all dressed up in fancy new clothes. Nails felt very elegant and proud leaving home. As he walked up to the school he was greeted by a tall, friendly young man who said, "You must be Paul Lewis, our new student."

"Yes, I am," replied Nails.

"Well, I hope you will be very happy here with us. I am Mr. Willis. I will be tutoring you in the evening at your home, so we will be seeing quite a bit of each other."

"I hope I will be a good student," replied Nails.

"I don't think we will have any problems," said Mr. Willis, with a smile on his face. "Come, I want you to meet our headmaster, Mr. Black, and your classmates."

As Nails walked into the classroom Mr. Black was in the middle of administering discipline to one of the students. A boy was lying across his school desk with his pants down and Mr. Black was hitting him with a long black strap. The blows were very hard. The boy being whipped said nothing, but only winced when each blow struck.

"Have you had enough?" said Mr. Black to the boy, whose cheeks were streaming with tears.

"Yes, sir."

"Let that be a lesson to you. You do your homework or you'll get it all over again."

"But - - - "

"I don't want any more of your silly excuses about having your homework stolen again. Is that clear?" said Mr. Black.

"Yes, sir," said the boy.

Mr. Black turned away from the boy. Perspiration was running down his face from the exertion of beating the boy, and his glasses were fogged up. Taking them off to wipe them, he saw Nails and said, "So you are our new student! Let what you saw be a lesson to you. We do not stand for any laziness in my school. You will face up or suffer the consequences. Is that clear?"

"Yes, sir," said Nails.

"What are you standing around here for?" Mr. Black said to Mr. Willis. "Get back to your class."

"Yes, Mr. Black," said Mr. Willis.

At lunch time in the schoolyard Nails went over to the boy who had been beaten by Mr. Black and said, "Hello. My name is Nails. What's yours?"

The boy, who was glumly eating his bread and cheese,

looked up and smiled. He said, "My name is Richard Towne."

"I felt awfully sorry for you, getting that beating."

"Oh, I'm used to it," said Richard. "See those boys over there — Clyde Marley and Steven Harris? They jumped on me on the way to school, stole my arithmetic homework, copied it, and then tore it up."

"Didn't you tell Mr. Black?"

"Yes, but he won't believe me. Clyde is his nephew and he will punish anyone who tries to tell on him. He thinks Clyde can do no wrong, and because of that Clyde is an awful bully."

"Well," said Nails, "if he does it again call me and I'll help you."

"Thank you," said Richard as they shook hands.

Watching Nails and Richard, Clyde and Steven started walking over to them. Clyde, speaking to Nails, said "Are you some kind of a foreigner?"

"No," said Nails, "I am an American."

"You talk awfully funny. How come?" asked Steven Harris.

"I don't know," said Nails.

"Look, what's your name anyway?" said Clyde to Nails.

"It's Paul Lewis, but people call me Nails."

"I'm warning you, if you start hanging around with Richard, you are going to get yourself hurt."

"I don't think you could hurt me," said Nails to Clyde.

"You don't think so? Well, take this," said Clyde as he threw a wide punch at Nails, which Nails easily stepped away from. Clyde lost his balance and fell on his face. All the boys had a good laugh at Clyde. Just then the bell rang and recess was over, so Nails and the other boys filed back to the classrooms. Clyde shouted after Nails that he was going to get it later.

That night after supper Mr. Willis arrived to tutor Nails. They went into the library and went right to work. In the middle of an arithmetic lesson Nails looked up at Mr. Willis and said, "Do I talk differently from the other boys?"

"Yes, you do," said Mr. Willis, "but it is not strange. People from different places, even in America, speak English differently, and it is true all over the world. You have an accent. You must have picked it up from the pirate you lived with. In a few years, Nails, most of it will be gone, so don't even worry about it."

With the lesson over, Nails and Mr. Willis went into the drawing room where Mr. Willis had a glass of wine with Colonel Lewis.

"Colonel," said Mr. Willis, "I would give anything to be in the army with you, sir."

"Oh, so you would like to be a soldier, Mr. Willis."

"Yes, sir, I would enlist tomorrow, but I have my sick mother at home to support and take care of, and I can't leave her."

"That's too bad," said Colonel Lewis, "but if you can't be a soldier, you are doing the next best thing. That is, being a good son."

"Thank you," said Mr. Willis. "My younger sister is getting married. I intend to ask her and her new husband if they would move into my house and take care of mother so that I may serve my country."

"I hope everything works out well for you," said Colonel Lewis. "If there is anything I can do for you, I would be most happy to do it."

Chapter Two

THE DAY arrived that Nails had dreaded. His father's leave was over. He would have to return to General Washington's staff at Cambridge, Massachusetts. Colonel Lewis, after having breakfast, stood in the front hall, resplendent in his uniform, and kissed Mrs. Lewis good bye. He stood back from Nails and said, "Paul, I guess I should not kiss you, you are such a big boy." He shook Nails' hand and said, "Take care of your mother. You are the man of the house now," and walking out the door, which John the butler held open for him, he saluted Nails. Then he grasped John's hand. "You take care of both of them."

"I surely will, Colonel, sir," replied John.

The Colonel mounted his horse and, at a fast canter, headed down the road.

As time passed Nails fell into the everyday routine of a schoolboy, except for the extra tutoring at night, his happiest learning hours. At school Mr. Black was very impatient with him and would deliberately ask him questions he could not answer. This made the other boys laugh and call him names like "dunce." This embarrassment spurred Nails on to find the answers and to work harder so that he would not be left open to ridicule for his lack of education.

Months flew by quickly for Nails, and he was kept up to date on how the war was coming by frequent letters from his father. Colonel Lewis wrote to Nails about the cannons captured by Ethan Allan and his Green Mountain boys from Fort Ticonderoga, and how they were hauled to Boston and secretly placed on Dorchester Heights to face the British fleet in Boston Harbor, and how the fleet promptly sailed away to Nova Scotia. He told about the American defeat in Quebec and the capture of Manhattan by General Howe's forces. He wrote that the army had retreated to New Jersey and that Washington's troops there had shrunk to only three thousand men.

Nails was now getting along nicely in school, the only drawback being the attitude of Clyde Marley and Steven Harris. Richard Towne had become Nails' best friend, and Clyde and Steven resented this because they liked to pick on Richard, but were afraid to because of Nails. One day everything came to a boil in a game of tag. Richard accidentally tagged Clyde too hard and Clyde jumped on Richard and started to beat him. Clyde was two years older than Richard and many pounds heavier. Nails, on the other side of the yard, saw the one-sided fight and rushed over. He pulled Clyde off Richard, whose nose was bleeding badly. Nails hit Clyde directly on the nose, knocking him to the ground. Just then Mr. Black appeared on the scene and shouted at Nails, "Stop that, you ruffian!" Nails tried to explain what had happened, but Mr. Black refused to listen. Instead he went into the school and came out with his long black strap.

Walking over to Nails he seized him and said, "Go into

the classroom, pull down your pants, and lie across your desk."

Nails said, "I have not done anything wrong and I should not be punished."

With that Nails broke away from his grip. The boys had formed in a crowd around Mr. Black and Nails. Mr. Black ordered the boys to seize his arms. Clyde grabbed one of Nails' arms and Steven the other, with Mr. Black helping them. Nails tried to break loose, but the three of them were too much for him.

Mr. Black ordered them, "Take him over to that tree, and pull his arms around it."

With this, Mr. Black laid the strap to Nails' back in a frenzy of anger. Even Clyde and Steven, who were holding Nails, were frightened. Suddenly Mr. Willis broke through the crowd. Seeing what was happening he rushed over and pulled the strap out of Mr. Black's hand. The two boys let go of Nails, who slumped down from the tree.

"Are you trying to kill the boy or discipline him?" demanded Mr. Willis.

Mr. Black said, "Willis, you mind your own business! As long as I am the head of this school we will do things my way."

The bell rang and recess was over. Mr. Willis went over to Nails and helped him up. "Are you all right, boy?" he asked.

"Yes, I am," said Nails, "although my back hurts a little."

Mr. Willis took Nails over to the well and gave him a

cold ladle of water to drink. Then he sent Nails back to his class.

Nails came home that night to a sad house. A letter had arrived from General Washington telling them that Colonel Lewis was missing in action and presumed captured. His horse had been shot from under him and he was last seen wounded and fighting on foot, with the British closing in on him.

Nails was close to tears. Although his back pained him terribly, he did not want to tell his mother of the beating he had received because she was so worried over his father. Nails told John about it and he took Nails down to the kitchen and fixed a poultice which he said was used to heal whipping cuts in the days when he was a slave, before he became a free man. It was very soothing to Nails' back. John kept saying, as he put the poultice on, "I ought to go up and take care of that man for doing this to you, boy."

Chapter Three

WEEKS passed without word of Colonel Lewis' fate until one day another letter arrived from General Washington, along with a copy of a British dispatch. The dispatch stated that Lieutenant Lewis, duly convicted of treason to England, would be hanged as of the date prescribed. In the letter General Washington said that the dispatch had been taken from a captured British courier. He said that Colonel Lewis had served as a Lieutenant with the British army back in England years ago. His discharge had stated that he was subject to recall in an emergency. With the war going on, the British had enacted the emergency clause in the discharge, and because Colonel Lewis was in the American army they charged him with desertion and consorting with the enemy. Both charges were punishable by death.

General Washington stated in his letter that Colonel Lewis was being held prisoner at the Wadsworth Estate at Farmington, Connecticut, that he had been badly wounded in the left leg, the bone having been shattered, but that he was being given good medical treatment by a local physician. General Washington promised that he would do everything in his power to secure his release.

Things were very glum at the Lewis house until a

man came with a letter from a Doctor Hawks in Farmington, containing a smuggled note from Colonel Lewis. The letter from the doctor told of the Colonel's condition. The Colonel was able to be up and around, but the doctor had been fooling the British about his condition by saying that the Colonel's leg had not properly healed, knowing that he would be promptly hanged if able to stand. Dr. Hawks thought that there was a good chance that he could help the Colonel escape if he had the assistance of at least two persons. He gave passwords to use if rescuers were sent and orderd his letter burned, saying that if it fell into the wrong hands it would mean his life.

Nails and Mrs. Lewis were sitting sadly, thinking about Doctor Hawks' letter, when Mr. Willis knocked on the door. "Lesson time again!" he said. Then he looked at Nails. "Why do you have such a long face?"

Mrs. Lewis handed Mr. Willis the captured British dispatch and Dr. Hawks' letter, which he read.

"Well," he said, "this is a real problem, but you have one volunteer to help Colonel Lewis to escape. I will be glad to go."

Nails leaped with joy.

"But what about your mother? Who will take care of her?" asked Mrs. Lewis.

"My sister was married last week and she is returning from her wedding trip today. They are going to live at my house, so Mother will not be left alone. I planned to join the Army next week anyway."

"Mother," said Nails, "I am going too!"

"Mrs. Lewis," said Mr. Willis, "I think Nails can help, and even if he should get caught, the British would not harm a boy."

"If I weren't so desperate I would say no," said Mrs. Lewis. "Paul, if I let you go, you must promise me that you will not take any extra chances."

"I will, Mother, and thank you! I promise we will bring Father home safe and sound."

"Well," Mr. Willis said to Nails, "we have our work cut out for us. First, you take a note to Mr. Black saying that you are going out of town to visit some relatives. I will have to get myself discharged by Mr. Black, and I am going to enjoy that. If I quit suddenly and you did not come to school, someone might put two and two together and figure that we had gone somewhere together. The British know that someone may try to help your father escape and there are many ears that will be listening for a plot to free him."

The next day at school Nails presented his note to Mr. Black, who said "I can't say I am sorry to be losing you for a while."

Later on in the day, during a history lesson, Clyde Marley picked up an ink well and threw it at Nails. It was just a bit of parting spite, but instead of hitting Nails it broke and splashed all over the wall. Clyde quickly reached over the shoulder of Jimmy Brown in front of him and took his ink well and placed it in his own desk. Mr. Black, who had his back to the boys, turned when he heard the noise, and saw the large black stain on the wall.

"Who did that?" asked Mr. Black.

No one answered.

"I can easily find out." He walked up the aisle and found Jimmy Brown's ink well missing. He grabbed him by the ear, threw him over his desk and then went to get his long black strap.

Nails said "Stop! Clyde did it and then stole Jimmy's ink well to cast the blame on him."

"You liar!" bellowed Mr. Black and struck Nails across the face with an open hand. Nails quickly ran to Mr. Willis' room, told him the story, and they rushed back to the classroom. Mr. Black had just set himself to strike Jimmy. Mr. Willis pulled the belt right out of his hand, almost knocking him down.

"What's the meaning of this?" growled Mr. Black.

Mr. Willis, with a terrific blow, struck Mr. Black across his legs with the strap. Mr. Black winced with pain. "See what it feels like to get hit with this instrument of torture?"

"You are discharged!" howled Mr. Black.

"Not before I tell you that your precious nephew Clyde is a troublemaker. No matter what he does, you will not face it. Instead you beat an innocent boy," and with that Mr. Willis threw the strap out of an open window, where it landed on a high branch of a tree.

Mr. Black was so embarrassed that he said, "Class dismissed for the day."

Nails met Mr. Willis walking up the street. He said, "Nails, I want to apologize for my actions of today. I lost my temper. I intended to start an argument with Mr.

Black after school over the beatings, and I knew that when I brought up Clyde's name he would discharge me. I did not intend to hit Mr. Black with that strap in front of the class, even though he deserved it. Well, Nails, I don't think we should walk any farther together. Remember, we are going on a secret mission. I will see you tonight at eight o'clock."

Chapter Four

NAILS met Mr. Willis at Perkins Crossroads that night and they rode for many hours before reaching the outskirts of Farmington. It was almost daylight. They decided to split up and ride to Dr. Hawks' house separately. Nails arrived first and got the doctor out of bed to give him the password.

The doctor said, "They have sent me a boy to do a man's work."

A few minutes later Mr. Willis arrived. The doctor was a little happier when he saw that Mr. Willis was a full grown man.

"Well," said Dr. Hawks, "I suppose we must work with what we have." The doctor then sat down and outlined his plan. "Today is Tuesday. We will have all this week to set up the escape. Saturday night most of the guard detachment comes into town to the local tavern to celebrate. There is only one man left at the gate and he is a very sleepy fellow. I have gone there on three different occasions on a Saturday night and he hasn't seen me walk in or out. The problem is inside the house, because Colonel Lewis is held in an upstairs room. There is a guard outside the door and at least three others spread out inside the house, and I can tell you, they are very alert."

"My plan is first to overpower the guard at the gate. Mr. Willis will slip into his uniform and sit in his guard box as a lookout. Nails, it will be your job to get a ladder from the barn and put it up to the window that I point out. I will help your father out the window and onto the ladder . You might have to come up the ladder to guide him down because your father is very weak from being bedridden so long."

As the week passed Nails and Mr. Willis took separate rides past the house, which was partially hidden by a high brick wall, to get the lay of the land.

Saturday evening arrived. Dr. Hawks, Mr. Willis and Nails had eaten very little for supper because they were so nervous, and the doctor kept fussing with his watch chain. Finally it was time to go. As they rode up to the guard house they could see the guard dozing as Dr. Hawks had said. His head was bobbing up and down. Mr. Willis walked up to him stealthily with his pistol drawn, took off the guard's hat, and hit him over the head, knocking him unconscious. He then stripped off the man's uniform and put it on. He tied and gagged the guard and hid him in the bushes, out of sight. Mr. Willis then sat down, with his rifle cradled across his lap, and put his head down as if dozing so that his face could not be recognized.

Things went smoothly. Nails found the ladder and put it up against the window that Dr. Hawks had shown him. Dr. Hawks walked by the guards inside the house, as usual, except for one who had the doctor look at his sore toe. The doctor promised that he would bring some medicine to cure it on his next visit to the Colonel and the guard was very grateful.

The Colonel was all ready for the doctor. He was fully dressed under the bed covers, except for his boots, which the doctor helped him to put on. The doctor walked Colonel Lewis around the room a few times and then said, "We do not have time for you to strengthen your legs any more. You will have to go out the window now."

The doctor could see Nails holding the ladder firmly as he helped the Colonel out the window. The Colonel was very shaky on the ladder. Dr. Hawks was afraid that he would fall off, so he motioned to Nails to come up the ladder and help his father down.

At the main gate something unforeseen was happening. One of the guards who had been to town had come home early. As he staggered through the gate, drunk, he waved at the dozing form of Mr. Willis and said, "Hi, Reg. You are the worst soldier in His Majesty's service," and he walked over to Mr. Willis, who rose to his feet, keeping his head down so that the soldier would not recognize him.

"You're not Reggie," the soldier bellowed. "Who are you?"

Mr. Willis swung his rifle at the soldier to try to knock him down, but the veteran soldier artfully dodged it and knocked Mr. Willis down. The soldier picked up the rifle, slung it over his shoulder, and staggered through the gate and up to the house. Mr. Willis, recovering from the blow, got up and started to follow.

The guard walked up to the ladder that Colonel Lewis and Nails were on and said, "What is going on here? Come down!" He started shaking the ladder when Nails and Colonel Lewis were only part way down. Nails, who was guiding his father's steps, lost his balance on the swaying ladder and fell on the soldier, who dropped to the ground, Nails on top of him.

In the meantime, the doctor had come out of the house, and seeing Nails on top of the British soldier and Colonel Lewis still on the ladder, rushed over to the scene. Mr. Willis, arriving at the same time, climbed the ladder and helped Colonel Lewis down.

Nails was still on the ground, with a look of pain on his face. "Doctor Hawks, will you please look at Nails?" said Colonel Lewis. "I think he is hurt."

Dr. Hawks helped Nails up, but he could not stand on one foot. The doctor felt it and said, "You have a broken ankle, Nails."

The Colonel said, "You had better tie and gag that soldier."

The doctor replied, "There is no need to. His neck is broken. He is dead."

Nails felt sick at the thought that he had accidentally killed a man.

Dr. Hawks said, "We must hurry and leave before we are discovered." So, with Mr. Willis helping Colonel Lewis and Dr. Hawks helping Nails, they hurried to their horses and rode off.

About five miles away they stopped at an abandoned farm house, where Dr. Hawks put a splint on Nails'

broken ankle and Mr. Willis took off the uniform he had taken from the guard. Then they rode on. Nails was in great pain and Dr. Hawks rode on the same horse with him because he was in danger of fainting from pain and falling from his horse.

Chapter Five

THEY rode all through the night and into the next day, avoiding all the main roads where there might be British barricades. They finally arrived at General Washington's camp at Valley Forge.

Nails was sick, and at times delirious with pain and fever, but in spite of all his troubles he was shocked at the condition of the men in the camp. The soldiers looked starved and most of them were in rags. Some had no shoes at all but had cloths wrapped around their feet. They were living in crude log cabins. The army was a sorry sight for Nails and the others to behold.

They were met by some of General Washington's staff officers who knew they were coming, for riders had brought in word of Colonel Lewis' dramatic escape. The British were scouring the countryside for him. They had put a 1,000 pound reward for him, dead or alive.

Nails was gently put on a stretcher by two soldiers and carried into a log hut. The doctor went with him, while Colonel Lewis and Mr. Willis went with the officers to see General Washington and make a report of the Colonel's escape. The hut had a dirt floor, but it was warm, and Nails was put on a cot beside a crude fireplace. A soldier brought over some hot rabbit soup and fed it to Nails. It made him feel better.

In a few minutes the door of the cabin opened and a large group of officers came in, including his father. Nails knew who the tall man leading the group was even before he spoke and introduced himself.

"I am General Washington. Welcome to Valley Forge, such as it is, Paul, or, should I say, Nails of Bunker Hill. We are very proud of you. I have an old friend of yours here who has told me a lot about you. I think you would like to see him."

Nails looked up. It was Mr. Baldwin, his "uncle" from Boston, who said, "How are you, Nails? You're up to your old trick of saving people from the British again." Nails laughed and began to feel much better. "I am on General Washington's staff, and many of the men we were with at Bunker Hill are here at Valley Forge, so you can expect a lot of company."

"Yes, sir, Major Baldwin," said Nails, smiling.

"Nails," said General Washington, "I am going to make you a Corporal in our army, if that suits you."

Nails beamed and said, "Thank you, General."

"Also, your companion, Dr. Hawks, is now a Captain in the Medical Corps, and Mr. Willis is a Sergeant in the Infantry."

Dr. Hawks said, "My first official act as a Captain in the Medical Corps is to ask you all to leave so that this young man can get some much deserved rest." Everyone left the cabin except Colonel Lewis. The father and son talked and reminisced a bit until Nails fell fast asleep.

Weeks passed and Nails was up and around and fit.

When he was able to walk, Nails noticed that the conditions at the camp were worse than he had thought at first. He wondered how an army could survive under such terrible conditions. It was now late in December and there were five inches of snow on the ground, adding to the general misery.

One day Nails was sitting on his cot, catching up on some arithmetic lessons given to him by his former teacher, Sergeant Willis, when his father stepped in the door and said, "You and I are having supper tonight with General Washington."

"That's wonderful," said Nails.

That evening Nails sat with General Washington and members of his staff at a large table in a farmhouse that the General was using as his headquarters. They had chicken for supper and Nails' plate was piled high with chicken and vegetables. In fact, as he looked around at the other plates, he realized that he was getting the lion's share of food.

"Nails," said General Washington, "we have been saving two very fat chickens for a special occasion, and your having supper with us is the occasion, so you clean your plate. Nothing will make us happier."

Nails did not need any more encouragement and enjoyed every mouthful of it. After supper, when the plates had been cleared, maps were laid all over the table and future plans were discussed, one of which was a surprise attack on the Hessian troops at Trenton at Christmas time when the garrison would be celebrating and off guard. Everyone agreed that it was a good plan.

Nails asked General Washington, "Who are the Hessians?"

"They are German soldiers who will fight for any country for pay," answered the General.

General Washington said, "We need a victory now to save our country, but there is one thing that bothers me about this plan. We have lost most of our contacts in Trenton. I received word yesterday that Andrew Blue has been captured and hanged. He was one of our best agents. We have only one more reliable contact there, but no way to get the information."

"Sir," said Colonel Lewis, "couldn't we send someone in to get in touch with this agent?"

"We could, but any strangers there are carefully watched. I don't think we would have much of a chance to make the contact."

"Sir," said Nails to General Washington, "what if I went? I don't think they would suspect a boy of being a spy."

"You're right, Nails," said General Washington. "I think you could do the job, but I would never send you on a spying mission, at least not alone."

Nails said, "General, do you remember Sergeant Willis who came from Philadelphia with me and helped save my father?"

"Yes," replied General Washington.

"If Sergeant Willis looked like a school teacher taking a student home for the holidays, I don't think the British would be apt to suspect us."

"You have a good point, Nails," said General Washington. "Colonel Lewis, would you allow Nails to go on this mission?"

"Yes, I would," he said.

General Washington then turned to his orderly and said, "Please have Sergeant Willis sent here immediately."

In a few minutes Sergeant Willis reported and listened to the plan to send them to Trenton to make contact with an agent. He said that it would be an honor for him to go.

General Washington thanked him and said, "You will carry on your own person any information you receive from the agent. I don't want to put Nails' life in jeopardy by having him carry any papers that might condemn him as a spy. Do you understand?"

"Yes, sir."

"If you get caught make sure that you say that Nails was only a companion and knew nothing of your spying."

"I understand," said Sergeant Willis.

Chapter Six

O N DECEMBER 24, just before dawn, Nails was awakened by Sergeant Willis, who said, "I have been told about the mission and our agent. It is time to leave."

Two horses were saddled outside the hut and they rode down to the Delaware River, where men were waiting with a raft to ferry them across to the other side.

They rode beyond Trenton and then back so it would appear that they were coming in from an opposite direction, rather than from Valley Forge. At the road block outside Trenton they were passed after being questioned. Nails and Mr. Willis repeated their well-rehearsed story of the school teacher and pupil on their way to the pupil's home for the holiday. Their story was accepted without suspicion.

It was quiet in Trenton, except for the Hessian soldiers who were celebrating the holiday in a loud and drunken fashion. As they rode in, Mr. Willis told Nails that they would meet the agent at the Snake's Head Tavern. "She is a barmaid. Her name is Mary Ann." Nails was surprised that the contact was a woman.

As they rode up to the tavern they could hear singing and shouting. Soldiers were staggering out the door. They tied up their horses and went in. The place was filled with Hessian soldiers; hardly a word of English could be heard. Nails and Sergeant Willis shoved and pushed their way to an empty table in a corner. There was so much noise that it was hard to hear themselves speak.

A tall, burly soldier was standing on one of the tables leading the crowd in German songs. Suddenly, spotting Nails and Sergeant Willis, he jumped off the table and came over to them, saying, "Why don't you sing with us? We are celebrating Christmas."

Mr. Willis said meekly, "We don't know the songs and we don't speak German."

"Well," said the soldier, "you will learn." He grabbed Mr. Willis and lifted him bodily onto the table and then he did the same to Nails. He said, "You will now sing to us. I will teach you the words. I am Sergeant Grumber, and I know all the words." He started singing in German and had Nails and Mr. Willis repeat what he said in German, singing to a melody. Everyone was laughing, some almost rolling on the floor. Nails could not understand what was so funny about their singing.

The sergeant, finding himself with an empty glass, stopped his musical direction and went to the bar for another glass of beer. Mr. Willis, who spoke a little German, explained to Nails what was so funny about their singing. The Sergeant had them singing German words such as "We dumb farmers fight with brooms, and lose our battles to dusty rooms."

"They are making fun of us," said Sergeant Willis. Nails' face grew red with anger and he showed it.

Sergeant Grumber walked back to the table and said to
Sergeant Willis, "You look as if you need a drink, my
friend." He then stood upon the table beside Nails and
Sergeant Willis and said, "Now a reward for our guests
for their singing." Then he poured his glass of beer over
Sergeant Willis' head and shoved him off the table. Sergeant Grumber accidentally tipped the table over, knocking himself and Nails to the floor. Nails and Sergeant
Grumber got up at the same time and Nails helped Sergeant Willis up. Then he turned around in a quick flash
of temper and kicked Sergeant Grumber in the shins.
The sergeant cried out in pain as he grabbed his leg.
Everyone in the room roared with laughter.

The sergeant was furious and grabbed Nails and started
shaking him. Two other Hessians rushed forward and
stopped him, saying, "You will kill the boy. You have
played your joke. Now you are paying for it."

Just then a young barmaid rushed up with a towel and
handed it to Mr. Willis. She said, "Dry yourself. Then
you had better get out of here."

While drying his head Sergeant Willis quietly asked
her, "Are you Mary Ann?"

She said "Yes — I know who you are. Walk out, drying yourself with the towel."

Nails and Sergeant Willis quickly walked toward the
door. Everyone was laughing. As they left, Mary Ann,
dancing with Sergeant Grumber, suddenly screamed,
"They have taken my towel with them!"

Sergeant Grumber said, "I will get it back."

"No, I will," said Mary Ann, and she ran outside and

met Nails and Sergeant Willis. As she took the towel she passed Sergeant Willis an envelope, saying, "Ride out of here as fast as you can."

Nails and Sergeant Willis had no trouble passing the road block out of Trenton. In fact, there were no questions asked at all because the guards were drinking and waved them on. When they reached the Delaware River the raft was ready, waiting to ferry them back across to Valley Forge.

It was early Christmas morning when they were presented to a just-awakened General Washington and his staff. Nails' and Sergeant Willis' report of the loose and drunken conduct of the Hessians, and the barracks and guard post locations given in the message from agent Mary Ann, convinced General Washington that the time was right for attack.

Orders were given to secure every available object that would float the army across the Delaware River. General Washington said, "The men may have to float across on the doors of their log huts." Word was passed around the camp and in the early hours it came alive with activity. The soldiers were making rafts and looking for boats along the river.

Later, Colonel Lewis said to Nails, "You had better get some sleep. We will not move until tonight and you will need all the rest you can get."

"Nails," said General Washington, "I want you to cross the river with me and carry our country's colors into Trenton."

"I appreciate that great honor," said Nails.

"You deserve it," said General Washington.

"Also, Sergeant Willis, I am rewarding you for a job well done by promoting you to Lieutenant."

"Thank you, sir," said Lieutenant Willis.

"Now," said General Washington, "obey your father and get a good night's sleep, or, should I say, morning's sleep."

Nails was tired and slept until the middle of the afternoon that Christmas day. When he awoke he smelled the aroma of rabbit stew. Then he saw Major Baldwin stirring a pot in front of the fireplace.

"Are you awake?" he asked Nails.

"Yes, sir," replied Nails.

"I'm the cook today. Get some plates and we will eat." As they sat and ate, Major Baldwin told Nails that all the boats and rafts were assembled for the crossing of the Delaware River, and from there it would be a nine-mile forced march to Trenton.

"We have ferried some horses across for the officers. We want you to ride, Nails."

"I can walk with the soldiers," said Nails.

"No," said Major Baldwin. "I know that ankle of yours is still sore. I have seen you limping at times."

"It is a little sore, sir," said Nails.

"We have been through a lot together, Nails," said Major Baldwin, "and this night, December 25, 1776, will be a day to go down in history if we win."

"I hope so," said Nails.

Major Baldwin then said, "Let us bow our heads and pray for the success of this night's work." They both knelt and prayed to God for a much needed victory. It was a prayer that was echoed through most of Valley Forge that day.

"Shall we go?" asked Major Baldwin.

"I am ready," said Nails.

Chapter Seven

NAILS was thrilled to be riding in the same boat with General Washington and to be carrying the flag. He could see his father in the next boat. The weather was terribly cold and it was sleeting. Then the boat started to leak and everyone had to start bailing out water. When they finally reached the other shore Nails' feet were wet and his gloves were frozen stiff. Mounting his horse, he started the ride to Trenton.

The weather got worse and the five inches of snow on the ground became crusted with ice from the sleet. The march was agony for the troops, most of whom had worn and torn clothing. Some had no shoes and their feet were wrapped in rags. The troops started to straggle and slow up. General Washington ordered his mounted officers to try to hurry and push the men on.

Nails rode back to the end of the file. He spotted one man, an older soldier, who was barely able to walk. He rode over to him and noticed he was shoeless. His feet had been cut by the ice and were leaving a trail of blood in the snow. Nails dismounted and said to the soldier, "Come on. Ride with me." The soldier gratefully accepted. Nails started riding along back to the head of the column. The area was hilly and the horse they were riding was slipping badly on the ice, and almost fell

down. The weight of the two riders was too much for him under these conditions.

Nails said to the soldier, "I am getting off. I have a cramp in my leg that is causing me pain. If I stretch it out and walk, it will feel better."

Nails took the flag, dismounted, and walked in file with the other soldiers, while the soldier he had befriended rode on.

Nails, remembering landmarks from his first trip, figured that they were over half way to Trenton. After walking a few miles he became very tired. His ankle hurt and his hands and feet were frozen. The weight of the flag he carried seemed to increase to about one hundred pounds. Nails closed his eyes at times and almost fell. He wished he could stop and sleep. He finally fell and two soldiers picked him up and, half dragging and carrying him, kept him moving along.

Reaching Trenton and seeing it put life, heart, and strength into the men for the attack. Nails, like the others, had caught his second breath. He unfurled the flag and rushed into the fray with the troops. The sound of the first shots at the guard posts woke the sleeping Hessians and brought them out of their barracks. Most were undressed and looked bewildered. Only a few carried rifles. Those alert enough to fire them were quickly shot at and either killed or wounded. The fight was soon over with only light casualties on either side, 30 Hessians and 5 Americans. It was a great victory with a small loss in human life.

The officers were having a hard time rounding up

over nine hundred Hessian prisoners and disarming them because many of the starving and frozen Americans had broken into the captured stores of food and drink and were making up for many a hungry and thirsty day. Finally the Hessian prisoners were lined up. They stacked their empty rifles and put their swords and bayonets in separate piles.

Nails, with a bugler and a drummer, walked over to a flag pole and lowered the British flag. Then, with a musical accompaniment, he raised the flag of victory over Trenton. Nails then walked past the line of Hessians. One of them reached out and grabbed his arm. Nails was startled and surprised. It was Sergeant Grumber. He held his sword, in its scabbard, in his hand.

Sergeant Grumber said, "I saw you raise your flag. You're a little soldier, but the last time we met I was drunk and tried to make you a fool. The winner is never a fool and you are the winner. I have carried this sword for many years. I have been a good soldier. Although I must give up my sword, I hate to throw it onto a pile on the ground. Please take it from me as a sign of an honorable surrender to the better man."

Nails, taking it from him, said, "It is an honor, Sergeant."

Nails looked up to see his father approaching.

"Paul," he said, "I have been looking all over for you. Are you hungry?"

"Yes, Father, very hungry."

"Well, come with me to the Snakes Head Tavern.

General Washington and his staff have made their headquarters there for a late Christmas feast."

Nails ate and ate until he thought he would burst.
Everyone was in a wonderful mood. General Washington
looked very happy and went from table to table to talk and
shake hands. After the meal was over General Washington
announced that he wanted to march the nine hundred
Hessian prisoners right through the streets of Philadelphia. He said he thought it would give a great morale
boost to his men and the rest of the country.

General Washington asked his quartermaster for a
check of the captured British stores. He told him to distri-
bute as many of the blankets, shoes, and boots as he could.
He said, "I want my army to be made comfortable and to
look as good as possible to the people of Philadelphia."

When General Washington's orders were passed, a line
of parade was formed. The General was at the head with
his staff of officers; then the American pipers and drum-
mers; next the Hessians with a single file of guards on
either side, with the Hessian fife and drum band in the
center; and units of the American army following in the
rear.

Marching into Philadelphia they were met by huge
crowds of people who had been told in advance that
General Washington was coming in with the captured
prisoners of Trenton. It was a proud day for Nails, who
was riding at the head of the column beside his father
with General Washingon's staff.

Nails noticed that the crowd that waved and cheered
them as they passed was very hostile to the prisoners be-

hind, and many tried to break past the lines of guards at their sides to attack the prisoners. Some of them were beating the Hessians. The situation became so bad that General Washington stopped the parade and ordered the officers back to help the guards.

Nails rode back with his father. He noticed that one huge man had pulled two Hessians out of the march and had pinned them down and was knocking their heads together. Nails shouted at the man to stop, but the man paid no attention. Afraid that he was going to kill them, Nails spurred his horse forward, drew his sword, and struck the man across the back with the flat part of his sword. The man, because of the stinging blow, fell back away from the soldiers, and the two Hessians ran back into the ranks.

The man stood up and, rubbing his back, said to Nails, "What did you do that for?"

"I thought you would kill them," said Nails.

"So what if I did? They are the enemy, aren't they?"

"Yes," said Nails, "but they have surrendered and they are under our protection. I think that if you want to fight the enemy, you ought to join our army."

The man said, "I don't know what your army is like, but you have spirit, little fellow, and you have talked me into joining it. You just tell General Washington that big Tommy Judge has just joined up," and the man waved and stepped into file with the guards.

Nails rode back to the head of the parade with his father and said, "I have just enlisted a new member into this army."

"Do you mean that big fellow that you hit with your blade?" asked Colonel Lewis.

"Yes," answered Nails.

"Well, I'll tell you right now, it looks as if you have picked a good fighter for battles, but I think that when the army is not actually fighting he will get into all kinds of trouble and spend a lot of time in the guardhouse."

Nails laughed.

The parade was now approaching his old school. Mr. Black and the students were in front of it, waving and cheering. As the parade reached the point in front of the schoolhouse the boys and Mr. Black rushed forward and surrounded Nails. This action stopped the parade. General Washington turned around quickly thinking that the crowd was after the Hessians again. He smiled when he saw that it was only Nails' school chums. General Washington passed the word that there would be a few moments' rest at that spot.

Lieutenant Willis came up from the rear ranks and Mr. Black shook hands with him and said that everyone had missed him and that they hoped he would be back after the war. Mr. Black pointed to a tree, and the strap that Lieutenant Willis had thrown on the branch still hung there. Mr. Black said, "There is my reminder of what I used to be." Lieutenant Willis shook hands with him again.

Nails, who was still on his horse, was completely surrounded by all the boys. Up in front was Richard Towne.

"How is school going?" Nails asked him.

"Fine," answered Richard. "Mr. Black is a changed man. No more strappings."

"That is wonderful," said Nails.

"What a beautiful sword," said Richard, looking at the German sword that Nails was wearing. Nails saw the expression on his face as he looked at it. He thought to himself, "I would like to give it to him, but I really don't want to part with it." Then he thought of the unfair treatment that Richard had received at the hands of Mr. Black and Nails blurted out, "Would you like it, Richard?"

"Would I like it? Do you mean that you would really give it to me?"

Nails took it off and handed it to Richard. All the other boys stared with envy. As Nails waved good-bye and the parade moved on, he could see Richard standing in the middle of the crowd of his schoolmates, proudly showing off his new sword.

Colonel Lewis rode up to Nails and said, "I am proud of you. I know how hard it must have been for you to give up that sword."

"Thank you, Father," said Nails.

As the parade moved outside of Philadelphia, Colonel Lewis said, "Nails, we are going to leave the parade now and go home to your mother. She knows we are coming. We are going to have a party for General Washington and my fellow officers tonight at our house." Nails was thrilled at the news.

The party was like a dream to Nails. There was an orchestra playing. The women wore elegant gowns and

the officers were wearing their best military dress. General Washington was sitting in a large, comfortable chair in the center of the drawing room, drinking a glass of punch and talking to everyone who passed. Suddenly he stood up and asked for everyone's attention.

"Ladies and gentlemen," he said. "First, I want to thank our host and hostess for this wonderful party. Second, I want to drink a toast to their son, the greatest little soldier in our army." He held his glass high and said, "A toast to Nails of Bunker Hill."

Nails blushed, but walked over to thank General Washington, who said, "Nails, I have been talking to your mother, and she has convinced me to put you on inactive duty so that you may continue your education." Nails frowned.

"Nails," said General Washington, "when the war is over we are going to need educated leaders, and with your courage and spirit you are a natural leader. Come," he continued, "I am leaving and I want you to walk with me out to my horse."

After he said good-bye to everyone, they walked out the door. Nails held his horse as he mounted.

"Nails," said General Washington, "if I need a good soldier for a special job, I know where I can find you."

Nails stood and watched the great man ride into the night. Colonel Lewis walked up beside him and said, "Son, the future of our country rides with that man."

As the figure disappeared, Nails stared into the moonlit sky and wondered what the future had in store for him and his country.